I Am Stumped!

By Lisa Rivard • Illustrations by Colleen Murray Fisher

I Am Stumped!
Copyright © 2012 by Lisa Rivard
Illustrations by Colleen Murray Fisher
Illustrations created with colored pencil, markers, watercolors, and acrylics.
Layout and cover design by Katheryn Hansen
Printed in the United States of America

Summary: When a young boy tries to play with his two friends, he finds himself left out and confused.

Library of Congress Cataloging-in-Publication Data
Rivard, Lisa
I Am Stumped!/Lisa Rivard–First Edition
ISBN-13: 978-1-933916-95-8
1. Juvenile fiction. 2. Friendships. 3. Elementary school. 4. Self-confidence.
I.Rivard, Lisa II. Title
Library of Congress Control Number: 2012931219

FERNE PRESS

Ferne Press is an imprint of Nelson Publishing & Marketing
366 Welch Road, Northville, MI 48167
www.nelsonpublishingandmarketing.com
(248) 735-0418

Written for my "best bud", AJ, his "lil man", A, and the
"very important" sea otter, Phil. May your dreams stay BIG
and your worries stay small.

A BIG thank you to my supportive family and
wonderful friends, especially Kathy Dyer for all her
creative efforts.

To the very energetic illustrator Colleen Murray Fisher, for
transforming these words into a visual masterpiece.

And to Marian Nelson and Kris Yankee,
for changing the world...one inspirational book at a time.

To Sean, Erin, and Maureen—with love. C.M.F.

"I am stumped, Dad! I always play with Brendon and Brody after school. Why didn't they invite me to come over today?" pouted Aiden.

"Oh, buddy, I can see you feel bad! Everyone feels left out once in awhile. I bet tomorrow the boys will want you to play again. Will you play a game with me today?" asked Dad.

5

Later in the evening, Aiden was still very bothered by his problem.

"Do you think my friends will play with me tomorrow?" questioned Aiden.

"Why don't you ask the boys what happened today? And if they still don't want to play tomorrow, I bet there are many other kids who would like to play with you."

Dad kissed Aiden's forehead and snuggled up with him in bed until Aiden fell asleep.

Ww Xx Yy Zz

rendon   Sidney   Brody

Addy   Aiden   Carson

ollin   Ethan   Sterling

Casey   Evan

At school the next day, the teacher asked the students to pair up with a partner. Aiden approached his friends.

"Sorry, only kids with names beginning with the letter B can be in this group," said Brendon.

8

"I am stumped," Aiden whispered to himself.

"You can be in my group, Aiden," said another classmate.

During art class, the teacher said, "Be sure to find a partner to help you hang up your masterpiece."

Aiden approached Brody. "Nope, already helping Brendon," said Brody.

"Not again!"
moaned Aiden.

At recess, Aiden ran to the monkey bars to climb with his friends.

"Only kids wearing blue and yellow are allowed to play here!" giggled Brody.

"Okay," Aiden said under his breath.
"I guess I'll play basketball by myself."

What did I do wrong? Aiden thought.

13

Ms. Match, the school principal, walked by. "Hey, Aiden, are you okay?"

"I am stumped! My friends said
I couldn't play with them."

"Did you ask them why?" questioned Ms. Match.

"No. I guess I should," Aiden replied.

At lunchtime, Aiden raced to sit down next to Brendon and Brody. He noticed they were eating the same thing.

"Only people eating veggie pizza can sit here," snickered Brendon.

"But I have nachos," Aiden moaned.

Aiden began to walk away when he remembered what both his dad and Ms. Match suggested. He turned back around with a sudden burst of confidence.

"I am stumped. Why won't you guys let me play with you?"

Aiden hoped one of his friends would say something to him. But neither one said a word.

He sighed and walked to another lunch table.

"May I sit here?" Aiden asked his classmate Addy.

"Sure," remarked Addy. "That would be great!"

"Aiden, I'm proud of you for trying to solve this problem yourself," said Ms. Match.

"Thanks," mumbled Aiden. "But they still won't play with me."

"I am going to talk to the boys. I expect much better behavior from my students. It's important to treat everyone with respect."

Ding, dong! The afternoon bell rang loudly.

"Aiden, would you like to stand in line next to me?" asked Addy.

"Thanks, Addy," said Aiden as he tried to smile back at his new lunchroom friend.

21

At the end of the day, the students boarded the bus. Aiden sat alone.

"Hey, Aiden! May I sit with you?" asked Brendon.

"Um, sure. But aren't you going to sit with Brody?"

"There's room for him, too," stated Brendon.

22

"You guys really hurt my feelings," said Aiden.
"I am stumped. Why wouldn't you play with me?"

"We're just good friends and like to play together.
But Ms. Match explained to us how we made you very
sad and that more than two people can play together.
I'm sorry for being mean," said Brendon.

"I'm sorry, too," said Brody.
"We won't do that again."

EXIT DOOR

STAY SEATE

BRODY

Tap, tap.

Aiden heard a faint tap on the school bus window.
Ms. Match was standing outside.

Aiden gave her a thumbs-up
and smiled brightly at her.

"Thank you!"
Aiden mouthed.

EAST LAN

"Hey, do you guys want to play at my house today?" asked Aiden.

"I do," said Brendon.

"Me, too!" exclaimed Brody.

"Cool! Addy is going to play, too!" said Aiden.

After school, Aiden was very excited to see his dad. "Hey, Dad, look who's here to play with me!" shouted Aiden. "This is my new friend, Addy."

"Hi, Addy," remarked Dad. "I am glad to see Brendon and Brody are here also. What was the problem yesterday, boys?"

"I'm sorry, Mr. Watson. I was mean to Aiden, and I hurt his feelings," said Brendon.

"We shouldn't have left him out," said Brody. "I'm sorry, too."

"Wow! Do you think we should celebrate your friendships with a treat for all of us?" asked Dad.

"Blue Moon ice cream for everyone!" shouted Aiden.

28 "That's my favorite!" yelled Addy.

"Here's to being great friends!"
shouted Aiden.

Dear Reader,

The old saying "two's company, three's a crowd" often rings true when it comes to kids playing. Two kids often pair up, leaving a third one feeling sad, confused, and even STUMPED!

Parents, sisters, brothers, other family members, and educators can help with friendship problems. They can give advice, mend hurt feelings, and help kids repair broken friendships. Adults can empower kids to be confident and teach them successful problem-solving strategies such as communicating problems, brainstorming solutions, and following through with a plan. Adults can also teach children how to be empathetic toward and respectful of others in their community by modeling those behaviors themselves.

I hope this book will encourage children to have the confidence to solve problems on their own or to ask for help from a trusted adult, if needed. I also hope this book demonstrates to all readers that as a society, we must be kinder to and more respectful of all.

Enjoy,
Lisa

Discussion Questions

Page 6
Why is Aiden so bothered by his friends?

Page 15
Why do you think Dad and Ms. Match suggested Aiden
ask his friends what was wrong?

Page 18
What does it mean to be confident?

Page 18
Why didn't Aiden's friends say anything to him when
he asked them what was wrong?

Page 19
How would you describe Aiden's new friend Addy?

Page 20
Why was Ms. Match proud of Aiden?

Page 24
Why did Aiden give Ms. Match a thumbs-up?

Page 29
Why is it important to be respectful of everyone?

Lisa Rivard was raised by her parents in New Baltimore, Michigan, along with her two sisters. Throughout her life she has enjoyed working with children in many different capacities including as a teacher, coach, and principal. She earned her teaching degree from Michigan State University and her administration degree from Oakland University. Most recently Lisa completed a PhD in instructional technology from Wayne State University. Currently, Lisa is employed as a Language Arts Consultant and assists regional schools in developing effective literacy plans. It has been Lisa's lifelong dream to become an author of children's books. For more information about Lisa, please visit her website, www.lisarivardbooks.com.

Colleen Murray Fisher is an award-winning illustrator and author. She has illustrated four books and wrote *The One and Only Bernadette P. McMullen* and *Miss Martin is a Martian*. She earned a master's degree from Michigan State University and teaches elementary school in Livonia. Colleen resides in southeastern Michigan with her husband, Jason, and their children, Sofie and Sam.